To my childhood best friend, Arán

Tundra Books, an imprint of Penguin Random House Canada Young Readers, a division of
Penguin Random House of Canada Limited

Library and Archives Canada Cataloguing in Publication

Title: My best friend / Miguel Tanco.
Names: Tanco, Miguel, 1972– author.
Identifiers: Canadiana (print) 20210090286 | Canadiana (ebook) 20210090375 | ISBN
9780735270701 (hardcover) | ISBN 9780735270954 (EPUB)
Classification: LCC PZ7.1.T36 My 2022 | DDC j813/.6–dc23

Published simultaneously in the United States of America by Tundra Books of Northern New
York, an imprint of Penguin Random House Canada Young Readers, a division of
Penguin Random House of Canada Limited

Library of Congress Control Number: 2020952292

Edited by Samantha Swenson
Designed by Alice Nussbaum and Talia Abramson
The illustrations in this book were rendered in ink and watercolors.
The text was set in Slimtype.

Printed in China

www.penguinrandomhouse.ca

1   2   3   4   5   26   25   24   23   22

tundra | Penguin Random House | TUNDRA BOOKS

My Best Friend

Miguel Tanco

I have a friend who follows me everywhere.
We give each other strength.
We have no fear.

My best friend is soft, warm
and comfy as a ball of cotton.

We never feel lonely
when we are together.

We have great conversations ...

Even if we don't always agree.

My best friend has a powerful sense of smell.

And great taste.

Sometimes too great.

My best friend doesn't like baths.

My best friend is my companion
in adventures...

And misadventures.

Sometimes we have to part for a while.

But we always find our way back to each other.

My dog is my best friend.

My best friend is my human.